The Adventures of Onyx
and
The Fight Against the Falls

by Tyler Benson

Ensign Benson Books LLC

Illustrations by David Geister
Design by Joe Fahey

The views expressed herein are those of the author and are not to be construed as official or reflecting the views of the Commandant or of the U.S. Coast Guard.

All characters appearing in this work are fictitious. Any resemblance to real persons, living or dead, is purely coincidental.

Ensign Benson Books LLC
PO BOX 609
Gloucester, VA 23061
www.adventuresofonyx.com
ensignbensonbooks@gmail.com

Printed and bound in the United States of America

First Edition

10 9 8 7 6 5 4 3 2

LCCN 2013955062

ISBN 978-0-9892846-2-2

This book was expertly produced by Book Bridge Press.
www.bookbridgepress.com

book bridge press[sm]

To my father and my mother, Tim and Joan Benson, for teaching me to *fight* for what is right, even against fearful odds! I love you both. Let the adventures continue!

—Tyler

"Attention on deck!"

Onyx and The Guardians of the Straits quickly jumped to attention as their new Officer in Charge approached.

"I am Senior Chief Connell and I want to welcome you to Buffalo, New York. I will be your Officer in Charge while you're all temporarily assigned to Station Buffalo."

Onyx watched as the tall Senior Chief walked up and down the line inspecting her and her shipmates. "With most of my crew rotating out this transfer season, I saw a perfect opportunity to put you all to good use!"

"Whatever we can do to help, Senior Chief," Dean said. "My shipmates and I are always looking for an adventure!"

"So I've heard," the Senior Chief said, as he kneeled down next to Onyx. "You must be the miracle dog that all of the Coast Guard is talking about."

Onyx barked back to the Senior Chief.

"Well, if it's adventure you want, an adventure is what you'll get! Station Buffalo is one of the busiest stations in all of the Great Lakes, and it's all because of one thing—Niagara Falls!"

Suddenly the search and rescue alarm sounded. The Officer of the Day yelled to the crew from the Station. "A 50-foot yacht with eleven people on board struck a reef at the mouth of the Niagara River. It's sinking fast!"

The Senior Chief looked at his crew. "Run for the boat! If that yacht sinks this won't be a rescue, it will be a recovery," he told them. "With the strong current of the river those people don't have a chance!"

The Guardians of the Straits ran to the response boat.

The Senior Chief told Dean, "You drive. I'll navigate."

Dean took the helm and yelled out, "Clear all lines and hold on! Coming up!"

The boat sped up, throwing the crew back in their seats. Onyx barked with excitement.

"It's a lot faster than the motor lifeboat!" Hogan yelled out.

"We're taking a shortcut called The Gap," Senior Chief said. "It cuts between two areas of shallow water, so it's very important to stay on track."

"Dean loves a challenge!" Evans said.

Dean spotted the yacht and brought the response boat alongside.

"Quickly!" Dean said. "Everyone off the yacht."

One by one the stranded people boarded the Coast Guard response boat.

Hogan noticed a young woman crying and hugging the rail. "It's time to go, ma'am!" he yelled, but the woman didn't respond. Hogan jumped over to the sinking yacht and grabbed the woman's arms. "We need to go now."

The woman held on tighter and kept crying, "I can't! I can't!"

The water rushed up around their legs as the bow began to sink. Hogan pled with the woman. "Please, you need to let go now."

Onyx had been watching Hogan and the woman from the response boat. Suddenly the dog jumped across to the sinking yacht. She nuzzled against the woman, comforting her. The woman began to calm down. Hogan felt her loosen her grip and saw an opportunity.

"Make you a deal," Hogan said. "You carry my dog, and I'll carry you."

The woman suddenly let go of the rail and grabbed Onyx. With all his might, Hogan picked them up and leapt for the response boat just as the yacht sank below the surface.

"Thank you," the woman told Hogan, as Onyx licked her face.

A Buffalo Police boat came alongside the Coast Guard response boat to transfer the people.

The Senior Chief yelled to the police, "We need to transfer these people quickly! We are being diverted to save a boat drifting toward Niagara Falls."

After the transfer, Senior Chief briefed the crew. "911 calls are reporting a boat drifting toward Niagara Falls in the exclusionary zone."

"Exclusionary zone? What's that?" Evans asked.

"It's basically the point of no return to Niagara Falls," Senior Chief answered. "You get into that zone, and you are going over the Falls."

"Not if we can stop it!" Dean yelled. Onyx barked in agreement.

As the response boat raced across the Niagara River, the depth alarm started ringing loudly, alerting the crew to the shoals, the shallow waters. Dean weaved in and out of the shoals using the chart plotter.

"A lot of boats strike rocks in the shallow waters and lose their propellers, leaving them drifting helplessly in the river," Senior Chief explained. "The one bad thing with this river is that the current is pulling them toward one of the largest waterfalls in the world."

"Well, Niagara Falls isn't going to claim anyone today as long as Onyx and her crew are here," Hogan yelled out.

Dean noticed a line of yellow buoys crossing the river. "What's that?" Dean asked.

"Here we go! Once we pass between those yellow buoys, we have entered the exclusionary zone of Niagara Falls," Senior Chief said.

"I have a visual on the boat!" Evans yelled.

"We need to work fast," Senior Chief said. "This is going to be a close one. Get the back deck ready for a tow!"

Hogan attached a heaving line to the towline on deck. "Ready on deck!" Hogan yelled.

"Making my approach," Dean said, as he positioned the response boat in place.

The stranded family waved and screamed in terror as they approached Niagara Falls. The depth alarm started ringing loudly again.

"This is as close as we get," Dean said. With all his strength, Hogan threw the heaving line to the family. A perfect throw, but it wasn't long enough and missed the boat by a few inches.

Hogan yelled, "We need to get closer!"

"We can't," Senior Chief replied. "If we get closer, this shallow water will destroy our engines and we'll be going over the Falls, too."

"I have an idea," Hogan said.

Hogan grabbed the towline and kneeled down next to Onyx.

"Okay, girl, here we go again!" he said. "We are as close as we can go, and it's up to you now."

Onyx looked into Hogan's eyes as he spoke to her. "We need you to swim this towline out to that boat, but I warn you," he said. "This isn't the Straits of Mackinac and this isn't the Gales of November. This is the exclusionary zone of Niagara Falls."

Onyx had never let Hogan down before, and she wasn't going to now! She took the towline in her mouth, stepped up to the side of the boat, and fearlessly leapt into the exclusionary zone of Niagara Falls, only so that others may live!

Onyx surfaced and swam with all her might, but she was suddenly pulled down by the might of the current. She surfaced again only to take a breath before she was rolled by the powerful Niagara River, tangled in the towline, and pulled down again. Onyx didn't surface, but the tension of the towline in Hogan's hand showed that she was still tangled underwater. Hogan saw in the crew's faces that all hope was lost.

Hogan looked at the family. He looked at the towline going below the waterline, and he looked at Niagara Falls growing closer. "My dog! My shipmate!" he screamed, and then selflessly leapt into the powerful current of the Niagara River. When he surfaced, Hogan grabbed the towline. With all his strength, he pulled hand over hand, making his way toward Onyx.

Then Hogan was pulled under.

Evans grabbed the towline and started to pull it in.

Suddenly, Hogan burst out of the Niagara River, choking on the water. He had the towline in one hand and Onyx under his arm.

The family quickly pulled Hogan and Onyx onboard. They attached the towline to their bow and waved to the Coast Guard boat.

Senior Chief and the crew couldn't believe what they had just witnessed. Without hesitation, the crew prepared the tow.

"All right then, let's get out of here," Dean said. "Coming up!"

The engines roared! The crew knew that they were in a fight. They were in a fight against the Falls!

The response boat with the family in tow slowly made its way out of the exclusionary zone toward a nearby yacht club where emergency medical personnel were waiting.

When they were safely tied to the dock, Senior Chief, Evans, and Dean quickly jumped over to the other boat. Onyx and Hogan sat, soaking wet but unharmed, surrounded by a relieved family.

Hogan looked up at Senior Chief and said, "You weren't kidding about having an adventure, were you?"

Onyx barked at the Senior Chief, agreeing.

Senior Chief laughed and said, "Welcome to Buffalo!"

Onyx and The Guardians of the Straits looked out over the river toward the mist rising above Niagara Falls. They all had survived another adventure. They all had survived their fight against the Falls.

GREAT LAKES AUTHOR **Tyler Benson** is from St. Louis, Michigan. He has served in the United States Coast Guard for more than a decade in St. Ignace, Michigan and Buffalo, New York. He began writing short stories about his search and rescue adventures in the Coast Guard to educate his three young daughters about what Daddy does when he goes on duty for 48 hours at a time. He wanted them to learn the importance

of service to their country and helping those in need. To help them better understand his job, Tyler wrote the stories featuring his station's morale dog, Onyx. These stories soon evolved into a dream—to publish a book series that would serve as a tribute and a way to bring recognition to all who serve or have served in the United States Coast Guard.

The Fight Against the Falls is Tyler's third book in the successful Adventures of Onyx series. Let the adventures continue!

www.adventuresofonyx.com